LITTLE LUV
Angel

Written and Illustrated by
Toby Bluth

Ideals Publishing Corp.
Nashville, Tennessee

ISBN 0-8249-8093-X

nce upo

NA TIME...

in the Kingdom of Heaven, there lived three little angels who were waiting their turn to be born on earth. The first little angel was named Faith. Faith was not at all certain where earth was; but she believed that it would be a very nice place. That's why she was called Faith.

The second little angel was a girl named Hope. She knew no more about earth than her sister Faith. But she wished it would be very much like Heaven, and that's why they called her Hope.

The third and smallest angel was a boy named
Little Luv. He was a funny little fellow, with big blue
eyes and a bushy mop of shaggy black hair. He wore
a baggy diaper secured with just one safety pin. He
had long ago lost the other one somewhere in the
vast infinity of Heaven. Everywhere Luv went, he
carried his empty baby bottle.

Luv had trouble keeping his halo on straight. And sometimes he didn't even bother wearing it. But the thing that set Little Luv Angel apart from all the other little angels was his heart. This was a great big valentine that he dragged around on a string so he wouldn't lose it. Luv's heart bounced along behind him, chipping and, frequently, breaking off in little pieces. He was constantly repairing it with patches because he loved it so. That's why he was named Little Luv Angel.

Faith, Hope, and Little Luv Angel were the dearest of friends. Luv had first seen the two little girls playing in a field of clouds. He walked right up, introduced himself, and showed them his heart. From that moment on, they were always together. The three romped and played together and waited for the day they would be born on earth.

One day, after the Heavenly Choir had finished its practice, the three little angels, who had been listening intently, tried to sing too. They started softly, then grew louder until they were singing at the top of their voices. Singing soon became their favorite pastime, and they sang all over Heaven. Even the members of the Heavenly Choir had to admit that when Faith, Hope, and Luv sang together, it was the most beautiful music in all Heaven.

Now, it was on the first day of spring in the Celestial Kingdom, all of the angels — young and old — gathered to polish and shine Paradise. Crowds of teenage angels jostled about, laughing and joking as they mopped the hallowed halls and walls. Others shook out the feather mattress clouds, giving way to occasional pillow fights with some of the smaller clouds. Older and more dignified angels polished the Pearly Gates, while cherubs dusted the countless stars. For Little Luv Angel, spring was an occasion to sing about, so he went off to find his two friends.

Together, the three little angels sang about
spring. They sang about the blossoms, the scents,
the sights, and the sounds. And as they sang, one by
one the other angels joined in until all Heaven
became one harmonious sound.

Suddenly, Faith spotted something and ran to
pick it up.

"Oh, look," she cried to Hope and Luv, who
both came running at once. "Look what I found!"

There in Faith's arm lay a pink rosebud, fast asleep. Faith thought it was the most beautiful thing she had ever seen.

"Wake it up," said Little Luv, "so we can say hello." (In Heaven, you see, even the flowers talk.)

"Oh, no," said Faith. "It's only a baby rose. It needs its rest. I'll just sit here and rock it until it wakes up by itself."

Little Luv suddenly had an idea. He whispered to Hope and they both giggled with delight at their secret.

"We'll be right back," they said. "We've got a surprise for you!"

Away they flew as Faith rocked and hummed to her rosebud. Soon it awoke. She gave it a kiss and it kissed her back.

"Hello, Faith," said a soft, deep voice.

Faith looked up to see an angel standing before her. She had never seen him before.

"My name is Guardian," he said. "It's your time to be born. I'm here to take you to your new home. I'm here to take you to earth."

Faith suddenly realized that her wings and halo had disappeared. She asked the angel where they had gone.

"Don't worry about those," said Guardian, "You've only traded your wings and halo for something better."

"What?" asked the child.

"For a mother," answered Guardian. "She's waiting for you now."

The older angel took the child's hand and, together, they started for Faith's new home.

Soon Luv and Hope returned, breathless with excitement. In their arms they carried bunches of baby rosebuds.

"Surprise, Faith!" they shouted. "Surprise! See what we brought you!"

There was no answer.

"Where are you, Faith?" called Hope.

"She went away," said a small voice. It was the baby rosebud. "She went away to earth to be born."

For a moment, Hope and Luv stood staring at each other. Then Little Luv cried out.

"No! No! She didn't even say goodbye!"

Hot tears filled his eyes as Little Luv Angel darted about in all directions.

"I've got to find her! I've got to stop her! Faith! Faith!" he called.

Little Luv flew around and around in circles, until he was tangled up in his heartstrings and crashed to the ground. There he lay sobbing.

Hope ran and put her own shaking arms around Little Luv, pulling him close.

"Oh, Luv," she said. "You've gone and broken your heart."

At that moment, Little Luv didn't care about his heart. He was only thinking about Faith.

Hope helped Luv patch his heart. It was heavier now as he dragged it along on its string, and Luv guessed this was because of the extra patches. Hope and Luv still played together and sang together. But they missed their friend.

Then one lazy summer day, Little Luv found two baby bluebirds. He brought them to Hope as a surprise. Hope loved the birds, and she talked and laughed with them for hours. (You see, in Heaven, even the birds talk.) They made her so happy she

called them her birds of happiness. Together, Little Luv and Hope built a nest for her birds. While Little Luv was gathering the last armload of straw to make the nest complete, Hope had a visitor.

"Hello, Hope," said a soft, gentle voice.

Hope looked up to see an angel she had never seen before.

"My name is Guardian," he said, "and it's your time to be born."

Hope, like her sister Faith, noticed that her wings and halo were gone.

Guardian told her, "Don't worry, you've only traded your wings and halo for something much better."

"What?" asked Hope.

"A mother," said Guardian. "She's on earth and she's waiting for you right now."

The older angel took the child's hand in his own, and together they started for her new home.

The two little birds saw all this; and they flew away to find Little Luv. They told him what had happened to Hope and the news broke his heart. This so frightened the birds of happiness that they flew away and were never seen again. As for Little Luv's heart, it needed more patches, which only made it heavier.

T.B.

Without Faith and Hope, Little Luv was so lonely
that he decided to run away from Heaven. He
would search the universe and find this place called
earth where his two friends were. Little Luv packed

his baby bottle, his broken heart, and some extra
patches. And one night, while Heaven slept, the little
angel silently winged past the Pearly Gates into the
vast blackness of endless space.

On and on he flew, searching the great
unknown void for that place called earth. Nothing he
saw resembled a place where his friends or anyone
else could live. He encountered a lot of dead rocks
floating in space, rocks that came from nowhere and
were going nowhere. On and on Luv went until he
felt that he could fly no more. Infinity was so large
but he was so small. His wings were just too tired to
go on.

Suddenly, a great storm broke all around him. The wind whipped at his face and the lightning blinded him. The rain soaked him through while the thunder frightened him. The storm ripped open his small bundle, flinging his baby bottle, heart, and patches into the darkness.

Finally, unable to go any farther, Little Luv collapsed in a miserable heap in the middle of eternity.

Ho, ho, ho," laughed a jolly voice. "What's this lying on my tummy?"

The little wet angel looked up to see a great face grinning back at him. Leftover raindrops from the storm trickled down the friendly face and splashed on Luv's head.

"Who are you?" asked Little Luv, who had never seen such a face before.

"Who am I?" repeated the face. "Why, I am the Moon; who are you?"

"Why, I am an angel," answered Luv, pleased to have someone to talk to again.

"An angel?" repeated the Moon. "That's funny."

"Why is it funny?" asked the angel.

"Why is it funny?" repeated the Moon. (It seemed to Little Luv that the Moon always repeated everything he said.)

"Because," laughed the Moon, "you look just like the children I see on earth."

"The earth!" cried the angel. "Do you know where the earth is?"

At that, the Moon laughed so hard that the child on his tummy bounced up and down 'til he nearly fell off.

"Do I know where the earth is? Climb up on my back and take a look for yourself."

The little angel climbed up the back of the Moon and perched on the tip-top. There, below and in front

of him, lay the earth. It was big! It was round! It was
beautiful! It was wrapped in soft blue clouds and
slowly turned as it waltzed in space.

"Ooooh!" said the angel. "It looks like Heaven."

"It should!" chuckled the Moon. "It was made by
the same hands."

Little Luv slid down the face of the Moon and
back onto his tummy.

"Please, Sir," begged Little Luv, "let me stay here tonight. By tomorrow I will be strong again. Then I can reach earth, please!"

Almost before the Moon could answer "yes" the exhausted angel fell asleep on his tummy. The friendly Moon chuckled and wrapped a blanket of stars around the sleeping child. Then he closed his own heavy eyelids and slept.

"Hello, Little Luv," said a soft voice.

Luv opened his eyes and looked up into the face of an angel he had never seen before.

"You shouldn't have run away," the angel said. "You had me very worried and I've looked everywhere for you. I'm here to take you home."

"No, please," begged the child. "You don't understand. I have to find my two friends, Faith and Hope. They're right over there on earth. I've come so far and now I'm so close."

Guardian smiled, "I know. But you don't understand. It's your time to be born. I'm here to take you to earth."

Little Luv was overjoyed. He jumped from the sleeping Moon into the arms of Guardian angel. Luv was not the least bit concerned that he no longer had his wings and halo. He was sure that they must have been exchanged for something much better. Something was probably waiting for him on earth right now.

"This earth," asked the child about to be born, "is it a nice place?"

"It's such a nice place," answered Guardian, "that very soon God will send his own little boy there to be born."

That's all the child needed to know. If earth was good enough for God, it was good enough for him. He hugged the older angel tight around the neck, and together they started toward Luv's new home.

And it came to pass, not long after, that God's little boy was born. His mother wrapped him in swaddling clothes and laid him in a manger where both shepherds and kings knelt before the babe. And to the manger that night, there also came three small children — a girl with a pink rosebud, her sister with

two little bluebirds, and their brother (not much older than the babe in the manger) bringing a great red valentine. Faith, Hope, and Luv gave the child their gifts; and then they sang a Heavenly song of peace on earth, goodwill to men. It was to be the very song God's little boy would sing his whole life long.